ISBN I 85854 549 8
Published by Brimax Books Ltd, Newmarket, England, CB8 7AU, 1997.
Printed in China.

Black Beauty

BY ANNA SEWELL
ADAPTED BY JOHN ESCOTT
ILLUSTRATED BY NEIL REED

Brimax · Newmarket · England

Black Beauty

Anna Sewell's Black Beauty was first published in 1877. It tells the tale of a horse born in Victorian England, and it highlights the harsh treatment horses often received at this time.

Black Beauty – a beautiful, well-bred stallion, starts out well in life. His first home at Birtwick Park shows how thoughtful and caring men can be to their horses. But Black Beauty's luck changes for the worse. He is sold several times, and each home is a little worse than the one before. He learns how irresponsible and heartless men can be. His mother's words to him as a young horse seem to ring true as he tries to comprehend human actions: "We are only horses, so we don't understand."

Black Beauty has several adventures and makes many friends as he moves from home to home. He realizes that not all men are bad and many do treat their animals with respect. At last he arrives at his final home – a place where his owners know the importance of kindness and understanding.

Anna Sewell wrote Black Beauty to draw the attention of the public to the cruel treatment received by horses. She did not live to see her poignant story achieve its great success – a success it still enjoys today.

Contents

CHAPTER I

My Early Home

The first place I can remember well was a large, pleasant meadow with a pond of clear water in it. Some shady trees leaned over it, and water-lilies grew at the deep end. Over the hedge on one side was a ploughed field, and on the other side we looked over a gate at our master's house which stood by the roadside. At one end of the meadow were some fir trees, and at the other end was a brook overhung by a steep bank.

While I was young I lived on my mother's milk, but as soon as I was old enough to eat grass, my mother went out to work during the day, and came back in the evening.

There were six other young colts in the meadow, but they were older than I was. We all galloped together around the field, but sometimes the others would kick and bite.

"They are cart-horse colts and haven't learned their manners," my mother told me. "You have been well-bred. Your father has a great name

in these parts, and your grandfather won the cup twice at the Newmarket races. Your grandmother had the sweetest temperament I have ever known, and you have never seen me kick or bite, have you? I hope you will grow up to be gentle and to do your work willingly, and that you will never bite or kick, even in play."

I have never forgotten my mother's advice, for she was a wise, old horse. Her name was Duchess, but our master often called her Pet. He was a good, kind man, and my mother loved him very much. When she saw him at the gate, she would trot over to him. He would pat and stroke her and say, "Well, old Pet, and how is your little Darkie?" (I was a dull black, so he called me Darkie.) Then he would give me a piece of bread, and sometimes he brought a carrot for my mother. I think we were his favourites.

I was two years old when something happened which I have never forgotten. It was early in the spring. There had been a frost in the night, and a light mist still hung over the trees and meadows. The other colts and I were feeding at the lower part of the field when we heard the distant cry of dogs.

The biggest colt raised his head, pricked his ears, and said, "There are the hounds!" Immediately he galloped off. The rest of us followed him to the top of the field where we could look over the hedge to several fields beyond.

My mother and another old horse were standing near. "They've found a hare," said my mother, "and if they come this way, we shall see the hunt."

Soon the dogs were all racing down the field next to ours, making a loud "yo-yo-o-o!" sound at the top of their voices. After them came people on horses. The horses were galloping as fast as they could. Suddenly, the dogs stopped barking and ran around with their noses to the ground.

"They've lost the scent," said the old horse. "Perhaps the hare will escape."

But the dogs began their "yo-yo-o-o!" again and came at full speed

towards our field, at the part where the high bank and hedge overhung the brook. Just then a hare, wild with fear, ran towards the trees. The dogs burst over the bank, jumped over the stream, and came dashing across the field, followed closely by the huntsmen. Six or eight of them jumped their horses over the stream and stayed close behind the dogs.

Before the hare could get away, the dogs were upon her with wild cries! We heard one shriek, and that was the end of her. One of the men whipped off the dogs, picked up the hare and held her by the leg. She was torn and bleeding, but all the huntsmen seemed pleased.

I was so astonished that at first I did not see what was going on by the brook. But when I did look, there was a sad sight. Two fine horses were down – one was struggling in the stream and the other was groaning on the grass. One rider was getting out of the water and was covered with mud, but the other lay quite still.

"His neck is broken," said my mother. "I cannot understand why men are so fond of this sport. They often hurt themselves, spoil good horses, and tear up the fields. And all for a hare or a fox or a stag that they could get more easily some other way. But we are only horses, and don't understand."

They carried the young rider to our master's house, and I heard afterwards that it was George Gordon, the squire's only son. He was a fine young man, the pride of his family.

Mr. Bond, the farrier, came to look at the black horse that lay groaning on the grass. He began to feel the horse all over and then he shook his head. "One of his legs is broken," he said.

Someone ran to our master's house and came back with a gun. Soon after, there was a loud bang and a dreadful shriek. Then all was still. The black horse moved no more.

"I've known that horse for years," my mother said sadly. "His name was Rob Roy, and he was a good, bold horse."

She would never go near that end of the field again.

Not many days after, we heard the church bell and saw a strange, black coach covered in black cloth and drawn by black horses. They were taking young Gordon to the churchyard to bury him. He would never ride again. What they did with Rob Roy I never knew; but it was all for one little hare.

I was now beginning to grow handsome. My coat had grown fine and soft and was bright black. I had one white foot and a pretty white star on my forehead. When I was four years old, Squire Gordon came to look at me. He examined my eyes, my mouth, and my legs, and then I had to walk and trot and gallop for him.

"When he has been well broken in," said Squire Gordon, "he will do very well."

My master said he would break me in himself, and he began the next day. To break in a horse is to teach him to wear a saddle and bridle, and to carry a man, woman, or child on his back. The horse must learn to wear a collar, a crupper, and a breeching, and to stand still while they are put on. Then he must learn to have a cart or carriage fixed behind him and to go fast or slow, whichever his driver wishes. He must never bite or kick or talk to other horses, and he must always do what his master tells him, even though he may be tired or hungry.

I had long been used to a halter and headstall, and to being led about in the fields and lanes quietly. Now, however, I was to have a bit and bridle. Those who have never had a bit in their mouths cannot know how bad it feels. A piece of cold, hard steel that is as thick as a man's finger is pushed into your mouth, between your teeth, and over your tongue; then the ends come out at the corners. It is held fast by straps over your head, under your throat, around your nose, and under your chin.

Next there was the saddle. My master put it on my back very gently and then made the girths fast under my body, patting and talking to me all the time. Then one morning, he got on my back and rode me around the meadow on the soft grass. It did feel strange, but I felt proud to carry my master, and he did this every day until I was used to it. Then he took me to the village where the blacksmith fitted my iron shoes. My feet felt stiff and heavy, but in time I got used to it.

There were more new things to wear. First there was a heavy collar on my neck, and then a bridle with great side pieces called blinkers against my eyes. With these on, I could only see straight in front of me. Next there was a small saddle with a nasty, stiff strap called a crupper, that went right under my tail.

In time I got used to everything and could do my work as well as my mother. For a fortnight, my master sent me to a neighbour's farm. The farmer had one meadow which was next to the railway. He had sheep and cows in it, and I was put in among them. I shall never forget the first train that ran by with a rush and a clatter and a puffing of smoke. I galloped to the farthest side of the meadow, snorting with astonishment and fear at the noise. But very soon I cared as little as the sheep and cows when a train passed by.

CHAPTER 2

Birtwick Park

It was early in May when a man from Squire Gordon came to take me away to the Hall. My master said, "Goodbye, Darkie. Be a good horse, and always do your best." I put my nose into his hand and he patted me kindly, and I left my first home.

Squire Gordon's Park surrounded the village of Birtwick. It was entered through a large, iron gate, and then you trotted along a smooth road between clumps of large, old trees to the house and gardens. Beyond this lay the home paddock, the old orchard and the stables.

There was accommodation for many horses and carriages. My stable had four good stalls and a large, swinging window which opened into the yard, which made it very pleasant. The first stall was called a loose box, where a horse is not tied up but left loose. It is a great thing to have a loose box. The groom put me into it and gave me some oats. Then he patted me, spoke kindly, and went away. In the stall next to mine stood a little, fat, grey pony.

"How do you do?" I said. "What is your name?"

"Merrylegs," he said, turning around. "I'm very handsome. I carry the young ladies on my back, and sometimes I take Mrs. Gordon out in the

low chair. Are you going to live next to me in the box?"

"Yes," I said.

"Then I hope you are good-tempered," he said. "I don't like having anyone next door who bites."

A horse looked over from the stall beyond. It was a tall, chestnut mare and she looked rather ill-tempered. "So it's you who has turned me out of my box," she said.

"I beg your pardon," I said, "but the man put me in here. I had nothing to do with it. I just wish to live in peace."

In the afternoon when the chestnut mare went out, Merrylegs told me about her. "Ginger has a bad habit of biting people," he said. "One day she bit James on the arm, and Miss Flora and Miss Jessie, the children, were afraid to come into the stable after that. I hope they'll come again if you don't bite."

I told him I never bit anything except grass, hay and corn, and could not understand why Ginger bit people.

"She says no one was ever kind to her before," said Merrylegs. "John and James do all they can to please her, and our master never uses a whip if a horse acts right. I am twelve years old, and I can tell you that there isn't a better place for a horse all around the country than this. John has been here fourteen years and is the best groom there ever was. And you never saw such a kind stable-boy as James. So it's Ginger's own fault that she did not stay in the box."

The name of the coachman was John Manly. He had a wife and one little child, and they lived in the coachman's cottage, very near the stables.

The next morning, John gave me a good grooming then put a saddle on me. He rode me slowly at first, then at a trot, and then at a canter. When we were on the common he gave me a light touch with the whip, and we had a splendid gallop.

As we came back through the Park, we met the Squire and Mrs. Gordon. They stopped and John jumped off.

"Well, John, how does he go?" asked the Squire.

"First-rate, sir," said John. "He has a fine spirit and is fast, but the lightest touch of the rein will guide him. They were shooting rabbits near the Highwood, and a gun went off close by. He pulled up a little and looked, but he did not stir a step to the right or left. I just held the rein steady and did not hurry him. It's my opinion he was never frightened or ill-used when he was young."

"Good," said the Squire. "I'll try him myself tomorrow."

I remembered my mother's advice, and the next day I tried to do exactly what my master wanted me to do. He was a very good rider, and when he came home, the lady was at the hall door as he rode up.

"How do you like him, my dear?" she asked.

"I've never ridden a more pleasant horse," he replied. "What shall we call him?"

"What about Blackbird, like your uncle's old horse?"

"No, he's far more handsome than Blackbird ever was."

"Yes," she said, "he's quite a beauty, and he has a kind, intelligent face. Shall we call him Black Beauty?"

"Black Beauty – why, yes, I think that's a very good name," said the Squire.

John went into the stable and told James.

"I'd call him Rob Roy," said James, "if it did not remind everyone of the past. I never saw two horses more alike."

"That's no wonder," said John. "Didn't you know that Farmer Grey's old Duchess was the mother of them both?"

So poor Rob Roy who was killed at the hunt was my brother! Now I understood why my mother was so troubled when he died.

A few days after this, I had to go out with Ginger in the carriage. I wondered how we would get on together, but she behaved very well and I found it easy to trot along beside her.

As for Merrylegs, he and I soon became great friends. He was a cheerful, good-tempered little fellow, and was everyone's favourite.

So I was quite happy in my new home. And what more could I want? Why, freedom! For the first three and a half years of my life I had all the freedom I could wish for; but now I stood in a stable, night and day, except when I was wanted for work. It was hard for a young horse who was used to galloping freely around a field. And sometimes when John took me out, I was so excited and full of life that I wanted to jump or dance.

"Steady, steady, boy!" he would say.

Then as soon as we were out of the village, he would give me a few miles at a spanking trot. Some grooms punished a horse for getting too excited, but not John. He knew it was only high spirits and could control me with just the sound of his voice. I was very fond of him.

Sometimes we did have our freedom for a few hours. This was on fine Sundays in the summer, because the carriage never went out on Sundays. It was a great treat to be turned out into the home paddock or the old orchard. The grass was cool and soft to our feet, and the air was so sweet. And we could gallop, lie down, roll over on our backs, or do what we liked.

It was also a good time for talking as we stood together under the shade of the large chestnut tree.

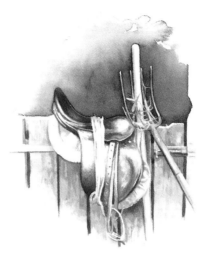

CHAPTER 3

Ginger

One day when Ginger and I were standing alone in the shade, she asked me about my old home and my breaking in, and I told her.

"Life has been different for me," she said. "I was taken from my mother as soon as I was weaned, and put with a lot of other young colts. There was no kind master like yours to look after me. And when it came to breaking in, that was a bad time for me. Several men caught me in a corner of the field, and one caught me by the forelock while another held my nose so hard that I could hardly breathe. Another wrenched my mouth open and by force put on the halter, and put the bar into my mouth. Then one dragged me along by the halter and another flogged me from behind. They did not give me a chance to know what they wanted.

"The old master, Mr. Ryder, could have done anything with me, but he had given up all the hard part of the trade to his son and another experienced man. His son was tall and strong, but there was no gentleness in him. They called him Samson, and he boasted that no horse could throw him. One day, he made me run around the training field on a long rein until I was very tired and miserable. The next morning he did the same again, and then he put a saddle and bridle on me and a new kind of bit into my mouth.

"The new bit was very painful and I reared up suddenly. This angered him, and he began to flog me. I began to kick and rear and plunge as I had never done before. At last, after a terrible struggle, I threw him off backwards and galloped to the other end of the field.

"I saw him rise slowly and go into the stable, but no one came to catch me. Time went on and the sun was very hot. Flies settled on my bleeding sides where his spurs had dug in. I was hungry and very thirsty. At last, just as the sun was going down, the old master came out with some oats. He spoke kindly and held out the oats for me to eat. Then he patted me gently and looked at the blood on my sides.

"'Poor girl!' he said, then he led me to the stable. Samson was there. 'Keep out of the way,' said the master. 'You've done a bad day's work for this filly with your bad temper. A bad-tempered man will never make a good-tempered horse, Samson.' He led me into my box and took off my saddle and bridle. Then he called for some warm water and a sponge, and gently cleaned the blood from my sides.

"After that, he often came to see me, but a man called Joe trained me. He was steady and thoughtful, and I soon learned what he wanted.

"After my breaking in," Ginger went on, "I was bought by a dealer to match another horse of my colour. But then we were sold to a fashionable gentleman in London who drove us with a bearing rein. You never had a bearing rein, but I can tell you that it's dreadful. I like to toss my head about and hold it up as high as any horse, but this rein keeps your head high for hours and hours until the pain is terrible. We had to wear two bits instead of one, and mine was so sharp it made my mouth bleed. Sometimes we waited for hours while our mistress was at parties or the theatre, and if we weren't patient the driver would whip us."

"Didn't your master care about you at all?" I said.

"Only about how we looked," said Ginger. "I think he knew very little about horses. The coachman told him I had an irritable temper but would

soon get used to the bearing rein. I was willing to work, but to be tormented like that made me angry. Then one day I kicked and reared and broke away from the carriage, and that was the end of that place.

"I was sold to another man, but he had a groom as bad-tempered as Samson. He always spoke to me in a rough, impatient voice and he would hit me across the legs with his stable-broom or fork if I didn't move quickly enough. I hated him! One day when he made me angry I bit him. He never came into my stall after that, and I was soon sold again.

"A dealer heard of me and said he thought he knew one place where I should do well. 'It's a pity that such a fine horse should go bad like that,' he said. And I was brought here not long before you came. Of course, it's very different here. But who knows how long it will last? I've decided that all men are my natural enemies."

I felt sorry for Ginger; but as the weeks went on she became happier and more gentle.

"I believe Ginger is getting quite fond of me," said James.

"Yes, Jim, she'll be as good as Black Beauty one day," replied John. "Kindness is all she needs, poor thing!"

Mr. Blomefield, the vicar, had a large family of boys and girls who came to play with Miss Jessie and Miss Flora. One of the girls was as old as Miss Jessie, two of the boys were older, and there were several little ones. When they came, there was always plenty of work for Merrylegs, as the children loved to ride him in turns.

One afternoon he had been out with them a long time, and James brought him in and said, "There, you rogue, mind how you behave or we shall get into trouble."

"What have you been doing, Merrylegs?" I asked.

"I've been giving those young people a lesson. They didn't seem to know when I was tired, so I just threw them off backwards. It was the only thing they could understand."

"You threw the children off!" I said. "I thought you knew better than that! Did you throw Miss Flora or Miss Jessie?"

"Of course not! I'm quiet and careful with them, and with the little ones. It's the boys," he said. "The other children rode me for nearly two hours, and then the boys rode me, one after the other for an hour, hitting me with a stick. Boys think that a horse is like a steam engine and can go on for as long and as fast as they please. They never think that we get tired. As one was whipping me, I rose up on my back legs and let him slip off behind, that was all. He got on again and I did the same. Then the other boy tried and I put him down on the grass. They're not bad boys and don't mean to be cruel, but they have to learn. When they told James, he was angry to see such big sticks and told the boys not to use them."

"I would have given those boys a good kick," said Ginger.

"I know you would," said Merrylegs. "But I'm not going to anger our master or make James ashamed of me. I'm expected to look after those children, and I will. You never had a place where they were kind to you, Ginger, and I'm sorry for you. But good places make good horses, and I wouldn't anger our people for anything! If I started kicking people, they would very quickly sell me, perhaps to someone cruel. I hope that never happens."

Squire Gordon was never cruel, and he would not stand by and watch others be cruel to animals. I remember he was riding me home one morning when we saw a powerful man driving towards us in a light pony chaise pulled by a beautiful, little bay pony. As he got to the Park gates, the pony turned towards them. Without warning, the man wrenched the pony's head around with such force that he nearly threw the little animal onto its haunches. Then he began to lash the pony furiously, holding it back with such strength that he almost broke its jaw.

"Sawyer!" shouted my master.

The man was a builder who often came to the Park to do work.

"He's too fond of his own will, and that won't suit me!" he said. "He had no business making that turn. The road is straight ahead."

"You often drive that pony to my house," said my master. "It only shows the creature's memory and intelligence. How could he know you weren't going there today? I've never seen such brutal treatment of a little pony. What will people think of you, Sawyer? You injure your own character as much as you injure your horse when you do it."

We went home slowly, and I could tell by the Squire's voice that what we had seen had grieved him.

CHAPTER 4

The Storm

O ne day in the autumn my master had to go on a long journey. John got me ready to pull the dog-cart then the three of us went off. I always liked to pull the dog-cart because it was so light and the high wheels ran along so pleasantly. There had been a lot of rain, and the wind blew the leaves across the road.

We went along merrily until we came to the toll-bar and the low, wooden bridge. The river was full and almost reached the bridge, and many of the fields were under water. In one low part of the road, the water was half-way up to my knees.

We got to the town and the master's business took a long time, so it was late in the afternoon before we started back for home. The wind was much stronger, and I heard my master say that he'd never been out in such a storm. We were beside the edge of a wood. The tree branches were swaying about, and the rushing sound they made was terrible.

"I wish we were well out of this wood," said my master.

"Yes, sir," agreed John. "It would be awkward if one of these branches came down on top of us."

The words were scarcely out of his mouth when there was a groan,

a crack, and a splitting sound. A big oak tree crashed through the other smaller trees and fell across the road right in front of us! I was very frightened and I stopped immediately, but I didn't turn around or run away. John jumped out and quickly ran to my head.

"What can we do now, John?" asked my master.

"We can't drive over the tree or get around it, sir," said John. "We'll have to go back to the crossroads. It will be a good six miles before we get to the wooden bridge again. It will make us late, but the horse is fresh."

It was nearly dark when we got to the wooden bridge. We could see water over the middle of it, but this often happened when the river was high. But the moment my feet touched the first part of the bridge, I was sure something was wrong. I stopped dead.

"Go on, Beauty," said my master, and he touched me with the whip. I dared not move. He hit me sharply, but I would not go forward.

"There's something wrong," said John, and he jumped from the dog-cart and began to look around. He tried to lead me forward.

"Come on, Beauty, what's the matter?"

Of course I could not tell him, but I knew very well the bridge was not safe.

Just then, the man at the toll-gate on the other side ran out of the house, waving a torch. "Stop!" he cried.

"What's the matter?" shouted my master.

"The bridge is broken in the middle," said the man, "and part of it has been carried away. If you come across, you'll be in the river!"

"You, Beauty!" John said to me, taking the bridle and turning me gently around to the right-hand road by the river-side.

It grew darker and darker and the wind got quieter as I trotted towards home. For some time, neither the master nor John spoke, but then my master said, "We could have drowned in that river, John. Men may be

clever enough to find things out for themselves, but animals know things without having to depend on reason. That's often saved a man's life, as it has ours tonight. People don't value their animals half enough, nor make friends with them as they ought to."

At last we arrived back at Birtwick Park, and the mistress ran out to meet us. "Are you safe, my dear? Oh, I've been so anxious!" she said. "Did you have an accident?"

"No, my dear," said my master. "But if your Black Beauty had not been wiser than we were, we would all have been carried down the river."

I heard no more as they went into the house, and John took me to the stable. Oh, what a good supper he gave me that night, and such a thick bed of straw! And I was glad of it, for I was tired.

One morning early in December, the master came to the stable with a letter in his hand. He looked very serious.

"Good morning, John," he said. "I want to know if you have any complaint to make about James."

"Complaint, sir? No, sir."

"He works hard and is respectful to you?"

"Yes, sir, always," said John.

"And he doesn't stop working when your back is turned?"

"Never, sir."

"And if he goes out with the horses, does he stop to talk to friends, or go into houses where he has no business, leaving the horses outside?" asked the master.

"No, sir, certainly not," said John. "And if anybody has said that about James, I don't believe it. I never had a steadier, more pleasant, or more honest young fellow in this stable."

The master smiled and looked across at James, who was standing in the doorway. "James, my lad, put down the oats and come here. I'm glad John's opinion of you agrees with my own," he said. "I have a letter from my brother-in-law, Sir Clifford Williams of Clifford Hall. He wants me to find him a trustworthy young groom who knows his business. His old coachman is getting feeble and needs a young man who will work with him and be able to take his place one day. How old are you?"

"Nineteen next May, sir," said James.

"That's young. What do you think, John?"

"It is young, sir," said John, "but he's as steady as a man and is strong and well-grown. He doesn't have much experience of driving, but he has a light, firm hand and a quick eye."

"Well, James," said the master, "talk to your mother at dinner-time and let me know what you want to do."

A few days later it was settled that James would go to Clifford Hall in a month or six weeks, and for the next few weeks he drove the carriage. We went through busy streets, and to the railway station just as the train was coming in and when there were lots of other carriages trying to get over the bridge.

At first, John rode with him on the box, and told him what to do, but then James drove alone.

The Fire

My master and mistress decided to visit some friends who lived about forty six miles from our home, and James was to drive them, with Ginger and I. The first day we travelled about thirty two miles. There were some steep hills, but James drove so carefully and thoughtfully that we were not at all harassed. He kept our feet on the smoothest part of the road and did all the little things which help a horse very much.

The sun was going down when we reached the hotel where we were going to stay that night. It was in the market place and two ostlers came out to us. The head ostler was a pleasant, active little man with a crooked leg and a yellow waistcoat. He led me into a long stable with six or eight stalls in it and two or three horses. The other man brought in Ginger, and James watched while we were rubbed down and cleaned.

"I thought I was pretty quick," James told the old ostler, "but you beat anyone I ever saw."

"I've worked with horses since I was twelve years old, and I can tell you it's a pleasure to handle a well-bred, well-cared for animal like this. Who is your master, young man?"

"Squire Gordon of Birtwick Park," said James.

"I've heard of him. He's a fine judge of horses and the best rider in this part of the country."

"He rides very little now," said James, "since the poor young master was killed."

"Ah, poor gentleman! I read about it in the newspaper. A fine horse killed too, wasn't there?"

"Yes," said James. "He was a splendid creature. He was the brother of this one, and was just like him."

"Pity! Pity!" said the old man. "It was a bad place to jump, if I remember. No chance for the horse to see where he was going. A man's life and a horse's life are worth more than a fox's tail – at least, they should be."

Later that evening, the second ostler brought in another horse, and another young man came into the stable to gossip with him as he worked. He was smoking a pipe.

"Towler, get some hay and put it down for this horse, will you?" said the ostler. "But put down your pipe first."

"All right," said the other man, and he went up through the trap door. I heard him step across the floor overhead and put down the hay.

James came in to look at us before he went to bed, and then the door was locked.

I cannot say how long I slept or what time it was when I woke up, but the air seemed thick and choking. I heard Ginger coughing and another horse moving about worriedly. It was dark and I could see nothing, but the stable seemed full of smoke. I could hardly breathe.

The trap door had been left open and the smoke seemed to come from there. I listened and heard a soft, rushing sort of noise and a low crackling and snapping. The other horses were awake now, and they could hear it too.

At last I heard someone outside, and then the second ostler ran in with a lantern. He began to untie the horses and tried to lead them out. The first horse would not go with him, nor the second or third. He tried to pull me out, but he was so frightened himself that he frightened me still more, and I would not move.

The rushing sound above grew louder and as I looked up, I saw a red light flickering on the wall. Then I heard a cry of "Fire!" outside, and the old ostler came in quietly and quickly. He got one horse out, and then another, but the flames were playing around the trap door and the roaring overhead was dreadful.

The next thing I heard was James' voice, quiet and cheery as it always was. "Come on, Beauty," he said. "We'll soon be out of this smoke." He took off his scarf and tied it lightly over my eyes. Then patting and coaxing, he led me out. Safe in the yard, he slipped off the scarf and shouted, "Take this horse, somebody, while I go back for the other!"

Windows in the hotel were thrown open and people were shouting, but I kept my eye fixed on the stable door, where the smoke came out thicker than before. Then I heard one voice above all the others and recognised it as my master's.

"James Howard! James Howard! Are you there?"

There was no answer, but I heard something falling in the stable. The next moment I gave a loud, joyful cry as I saw James coming through the smoke, leading Ginger with him.

"My brave lad!" said the master. "Are you hurt?" James shook his head, for he could not speak.

Suddenly, I heard the sound of wheels and galloping horses. "It's the fire engine!" shouted someone. "Stand back!"

Two horses dashed into the yard with the heavy fire engine behind them. The firemen leaped out, and we went quickly into the broad, quiet market place.

The master led us to a large hotel on the other side. As soon as the ostler came, he hurried off to find his wife.

The next morning, he came to see how we were and to speak to James. I did not hear much, but I could see that James looked very happy, and I thought the master was proud of him.

At first, no one could guess what caused the fire, but then a man said that he saw Dick Towler go into the stable smoking a pipe. When Dick came out again he didn't have his pipe. The second ostler told how he asked Dick to go up the ladder to put down some hay, but also told him to put down his pipe first. Dick denied taking the pipe with him, but nobody believed him. I remembered John Manly's rule to never allow a pipe in the stable, and I thought it ought to be a rule everywhere.

James said the roof and floor had all fallen in and that only the black walls were standing. Two poor horses who could not get out were buried under the burnt rafters and tiles.

Joe Green

The rest of our journey was very easy, and a little after sunset we reached the house of my master's friend. A kind coachman made us comfortable in a clean, snug stable, and we stayed two or three days before returning home.

"I wonder who is coming in my place," said James.

"Little Joe Green," said John.

"But he's only a child," said James.

"He's fourteen and a half, but he's quick and willing, and kind-hearted too. I've agreed to try him for six weeks."

The next day, Joe Green came to learn all he could before James left. He was a happy little fellow and always came whistling to his work.

At last the day came when James had to leave us, and he looked quite down-hearted that morning. "I'm leaving a great deal behind," he said to John. "My mother and Betsy, you, a good master and mistress, and the horses. And I shan't know a soul at the new place."

"Cheer up," said John. "You'll make friends there, and if you get on well – as I'm sure you will – your mother will be proud of you."

So John cheered him up, but everyone was sorry to lose James.

One night, a few days after James had left, I was awakened by the stable bell ringing loudly. I heard the door of John's house open, and his feet running up to the Hall. He was back quickly.

He unlocked the stable door and ran in calling, "Wake up, Beauty!" And before I could think, he had the saddle on my back and the bridle on my head.

The master was waiting at the Hall door. "Ride for your life, John," he said, "or for your mistress' life. There's not a moment to lose. Give this note to Dr. White, then rest your horse at the inn and be back again as soon as you can."

Away went John and I, through the Park, through the village, and down the hill. There was a long piece of level road by the river-side, and John said, "Now, Beauty, do your best!" And so I did. I wanted no whip or spur, and for two miles I galloped as fast as I could lay my feet to the ground. My grandfather who won the race at Newmarket could not have gone faster. When we came to the bridge, John pulled me up a little and patted my neck. "Well done, Beauty! Good old fellow," he said.

Then I was off again as fast as before. The air was frosty and the moon was bright, and it was very pleasant. We went through a village and a dark wood, then uphill, and downhill. After eight miles, we came to the town, and went through the streets and into the market place.

The church clock struck three as we drew up outside Dr. White's door. John rang the bell twice, then knocked at the door like thunder. A window was pushed up and Dr. White's head appeared, wearing a nightcap. "What do you want?" he said.

"Mrs. Gordon is very ill, sir," said John. "You must come at once, or she'll die. Here's a note."

The doctor was soon at the door. "My horse has been out all day and is worn out. Can I take yours?"

"He's galloped nearly all the way, sir, and I was to give him a rest, but I think my master would not be against it," said John.

"I'll soon be ready," said the doctor.

John stood by me and stroked my neck. I was very hot. The doctor came out with his riding whip.

"You won't need that, sir," said John. "Black Beauty will go until he drops. Take care of him, sir, if you can."

The doctor was a heavier man than John, and was not as good a rider, but I did my very best. Joe was waiting at the gate and the master was at the Hall door. He did not speak, and the doctor went into the house with him. Joe led me to the stable.

My legs shook under me and I could only stand and pant. There was not a dry hair on my body, and water ran down my legs. I steamed all over. Poor Joe! He was young and knew very little, but I am sure he did the best he could. He rubbed my legs and my chest, but he did not put a warm cloth on me. He thought I was hot and would not like it. Then he gave me a pail of water to drink, then some hay and some corn and, thinking he had done right, he went away.

Soon I began to shake and tremble, and turned deadly cold. My legs and my chest ached and I felt sore all over. Oh, how I wished for my warm, thick cloth, and for John, but he had eight miles to walk. I lay down in my straw and tried to sleep.

After a long time, I heard John at the door. I gave a low moan, and he was at my side in a moment. I could not tell him how I felt, but he seemed to know. He covered me with three warm cloths then he ran for some hot water. He made me some warm gruel which I drank. Then I went to sleep.

"Stupid boy!" John said over and over again. "No cloth put on, and I dare say the water was cold too. Boys are no good!"

I was now very ill. A strong inflammation had attacked my lungs and I could not draw breath without pain. John nursed me night and day, and my master often came to see me too.

"My poor Beauty," he said one day. "My good horse, you saved your mistress's life, Beauty! Yes, you saved her life."

I was very glad to hear that. John told my master that he never saw a horse go so fast.

One night, Tom Green came to help John give me my medicine, then stayed for a while. At first both men were silent. Then Tom said, "I wish, John, you'd say a kind word to Joe. The boy is heart-broken; he can't eat his meals or smile. He knows it's his fault, but he did his best. He says if Beauty dies no one will ever speak to him again. But he's not a bad boy."

After a short pause John said, "I know he meant no harm, but that horse is the pride of my heart and a favourite of the master and mistress. To think that his life may be thrown away like this is more than I can bear. But I'll give the boy a kind word tomorrow if Beauty is better."

I heard no more of this conversation, for the medicine did well and made me sleep. In the morning, I felt much better.

Joe Green learned his duties quickly, and was so careful that John began to trust him with many things. One morning John was out, and the master wanted a note taken immediately to a gentleman's house about three miles away. He sent orders for Joe to saddle me and take it.

The note was delivered, and we were returning through a brickfield when we saw a cart heavily loaded with bricks. The wheels had stuck fast

in the stiff, muddy ruts. The carter was shouting and flogging the two horses unmercifully.

"Don't flog the horses like that," said Joe. "The wheels are stuck. I'll help you lighten the cart."

"Mind your own business, you impudent young rascal, and I'll mind mine!" said the man.

Joe turned my head, and we galloped towards the house of the master brickmaker, Mr. Clay. Joe knocked on the door.

The door opened. "Hello, young man," began Mr. Clay.

"There's a fellow in your brickfield flogging two horses to death!" Joe told him, his voice shaking with anger. "I told him to stop, but he wouldn't. I offered to help him lighten the cart, but he refused. I think he's drunk. Please go, sir!"

"Thank you," said the man, running for his hat. "Will you give evidence if I bring the fellow up before a magistrate?"

"I'll be happy to," said Joe.

When we got home, Joe told John.

"You did right, Joe," said John. "Many folks would have ridden by and thought 'twas none of their business to interfere. But cruelty is everybody's business."

Just before dinner, the master sent for Joe. The drunken man was accused of cruelty to horses and Joe was wanted to give evidence. We heard afterwards that the poor horses were so exhausted and so badly beaten that the carter was sent for trial and might be sentenced to two or three months in prison.

Joe came across and gave me a friendly slap. "We won't see such things done, will we, old fellow?" he said.

And he seemed to have grown up suddenly.

CHAPTER 7

Earlshall Park

I had now lived at this place for three happy years, but sad changes were about to come over us. We heard from time to time that our mistress was ill, and the doctor was often at the house. Then we heard that she must leave her home and go to a warm country for two or three years. Everybody was sorry, but the master immediately started making arrangements to leave England.

John was silent and sad, and Joe scarcely whistled. Then we heard that the master had sold Ginger and me to an old friend of his, Lord Westerleigh, Merrylegs was given to Mr. Blomefield, and Joe was engaged to take care of him. John was offered several good places but wanted to wait and look around.

"I want to train young horses," he told the master.

"I cannot think of anyone more suitable for that work than you, John," said the master. "You understand horses, and somehow they understand you. If I can help you in any way, write to me."

The next morning, John took Ginger and me across country about fifteen miles to Earlshall Park where Lord Westerleigh lived. There was a very fine house and lots of stables. We went through a stone gateway and

John asked for Mr. York.

Mr. York was a fine-looking, middle-aged man with a voice that expected to be obeyed. He called a groom to take us to our boxes, then invited John to take some refreshment. We were taken to a light, airy stable and placed in boxes next to one another, where we were rubbed down and fed. Half an hour later, John and Mr. York, who was to be our new coachman, came in to see us.

Mr. York looked at us carefully. "Is there anything you want to mention about them, Mr. Manly?" he said.

"I don't believe there's a better pair of horses in the country," said John, "but they're not alike. The black one has the most perfect temperament I've ever known. But I fancy the chestnut must have had bad treatment. She came to us snappish and suspicious, but she has grown better-tempered in the last three years. We've never used a bearing rein with either of them."

"They must wear one here," said York. "I prefer a loose rein myself, but her ladyship follows the fashion. If her horses are not reined up tight, she won't look at them."

John came to pat and speak to each of us for the last time. I held my face close to him, which was all I could do to say goodbye, and then he was gone. I have never seen him since.

Lord Westerleigh came to look at us the next day and seemed pleased.

"Keep an eye on the mare," he told York. "Put the bearing rein on easy at first, and I'll mention it to your lady."

In the afternoon, we were harnessed and put in the carriage and led to the front of the house. Her ladyship came out and looked at us. She was a tall, proud-looking woman and did not look pleased. But she said nothing and got into the carriage.

It was my first time to wear the bearing-rein, and it certainly was a nuisance not to be able to get my head down now and then. I felt anxious

about Ginger, but she seemed to be quiet and content.

But the next afternoon when her ladyship came down the steps, she said, "York, you must put those horses' heads higher. They are not fit to be seen."

"I beg your pardon, my lady," said York, "but they have not been reined up for three years. His lordship said it would be safer to bring them up a little at a time. But if it pleases your ladyship, I can take them up a little more."

"Do so," she said.

That day we had a steep hill to go up. I wanted to put my head forward to make it easier, but I couldn't.

"Now you see what it's like," said Ginger. "If it doesn't get much worse, I shall say nothing. But if they rein me up tight, why, let 'em look out! I can't bear it, and I won't!"

Each day the bearing-reins were shortened. Then one day her ladyship came out later than usual and said, "Are you never going to get those horses' heads up, York? Raise them at once, and let's have no more of this nonsense."

York came to me first and fixed the rein so tight that it was almost intolerable. Then he went to Ginger. But the moment he took off the rein, she reared up on her back legs, then kicked herself out of the carriage and fell down, giving me a severe blow as she went. York sat on her head to keep her still and shouted, "Unbuckle the black horse! Unscrew the carriage pole! Cut the trace!"

The groom set me free, led me to my box, and then ran back to York. I was angry and my leg was sore. I felt like kicking the first person who came near me.

Before long, Ginger was led in by two grooms. York was with her and came to look at me.

"Confound those bearing reins!" he said to himself. "I knew they would cause trouble." He saw where I had been kicked and sponged it gently with hot water and put on some lotion.

The master blamed York for taking orders from the mistress, and York said that in future he would take orders only from his lordship. But things went on the same as before, except that Ginger was never put into the carriage again. I had a fresh partner called Max who had always been used to the tight rein.

What I suffered those four months pulling her ladyship's carriage would be hard to describe. The sharp bit cut into my tongue, making me foam at the mouth, and I felt worn and depressed. In my old home I always knew that John and my master were my friends, but here I had no friend. York knew how the rein harassed me, but he did nothing about it.

In the spring, Lord Westerleigh and part of his family went up to London and took York with them. Lady Harriet, who remained at the Hall,

never went out in the carriage, and Lady Anne preferred riding on horseback with her brother or cousins. She chose me for her horse and I enjoyed these rides. Sometimes I was with Ginger, sometimes with Lizzie, a horse liked by the young gentlemen.

A gentleman called Blantyre was staying at the Hall. He always rode Lizzie and was so pleased with her that Lady Anne wanted to try her.

"I don't advise it," said Blantyre. "She is a charming creature, but she is too nervous for a young lady."

"My dear cousin," said Lady Anne, laughing, "I've been riding horses since I was a baby and have followed the hounds many times. I intend to try Lizzie, so help me up."

There was no more to be said. He placed her carefully into the side-saddle, and then mounted me. Just as we were moving off, Lady Harriet asked for a note to be taken to Dr. Ashley in the village.

The village was about a mile away, and the doctor's house was the last one in it. Blantyre got off to open the gate for Lady Anne but she said, "I'll wait here for you."

He looked doubtful but went off.

There was a meadow on the opposite side of the road, and the gate was open. Just then, some cart-horses and several young colts came trotting out. There was a boy behind them, cracking a great whip. The colts were wild and excited, and suddenly one of them bolted across the road and blundered up against Lizzie's back legs. She gave a violent kick and galloped off.

I gave a loud neigh for help, pawing the ground with my foot until Mr. Blantyre came running to the gate. He caught sight of the flying figure, now far away on the road. In an instant, he sprang into the saddle and we dashed after them.

For about a mile and a half the road was straight. Then it bent to the right before becoming two roads. Long before we came to the bend, Lizzie

was out of sight. Which way had she turned? A woman was in her garden, looking up the road. "Which way?" shouted Blantyre.

"To the right!" cried the woman, pointing.

Away we went, up the right-hand road. We saw Lizzie for a moment, then she was gone again. Several times we caught glimpses, but lost her again. Then we were on the common, and on very rough ground, the worst place for galloping.

We saw them flying ahead of us. My lady's hat was gone and her long brown hair was streaming behind her. About half-way across the heath there was a wide dyke, recently cut. The earth from it was heaped on the other side. Surely this would stop them! But with scarcely a pause, Lizzie took the leap, stumbled among the heaped earth, and fell.

I cleared both the dyke and bank and landed safely. Lady Anne was lying motionless on the ground. Blantyre kneeled beside her and called her name, but there was no reply. Her face was a ghastly white and her eyes were closed.

"Annie, dear Annie, do speak!" he cried.

Two men were cutting turf close by and they ran across.

"Can you ride?" Blantyre asked one of them.

"I'm not much of a horseman, sir," he said. "But I'll risk my neck for the Lady Anne."

"Mount this horse," said Blantyre. "Your neck will be quite safe with him. Ride to the doctor and ask him to come immediately, then go on to the Hall. Tell them all you know and ask them to send a carriage."

The man scrambled into my saddle and we galloped off.

There was a great deal of hurry and excitement at the Hall when the news became known. I was put into my box. The saddle and bridle were taken off and a cloth was thrown over me.

Two days later Blantyre paid me a visit, patting and praising me. "I'm sure you knew Annie was in danger," he said. "She must ride only you from now on."

I was just glad to know that my young mistress was out of danger and would soon be able to ride again.

CHAPTER 8

Reuben Smith

A man called Reuben Smith was left in charge of the stables when York went to London. He was gentle and clever with horses, and was a first-rate driver. But he had one great fault, and that was his love of drink. He used to stay sober for weeks or months, but then he would break out and have a "bout" of it, as York called it. He would be a disgrace to himself and a terror to his wife and children. As he was a useful man, York kept quiet about Smith's drinking, saying nothing to his lordship. Then one night Smith drove some ladies and gentlemen home from a party and was so drunk that he could not hold the reins. Of course, this could not be hidden and Smith was dismissed at once.

But shortly before Ginger and I came, Smith was taken back again. York had spoken to the Earl, who is a very kind-hearted man, and Smith had promised never to get drunk again. He had kept his promise so well that it was thought he might be trusted to look after the stables while York was away.

It was early April and the light brougham was to be smartened up. It was arranged that Smith should take it to town and leave it at the carriage-maker's, then ride me back again. As Mr. Blantyre wanted to go to the station, he came with us.

At the station, Mr. Blantyre gave Smith some money and said, "Take care of Lady Anne and don't let her horse be hacked about by any young rascal who wants to ride him. Keep him for the lady."

We left the carriage at the maker's, and Smith rode me to the White Lion. He ordered the ostler to feed me well and have me ready at four o'clock. One of my front shoes was loose, but the stable-man did not see it until four o'clock. Smith came back at five and said he would now leave at six because he'd met some old friends. The stable-man told him about the loose shoe.

"It'll be all right until we get home," said Smith.

He did not come back at six, nor seven, nor eight, and it was nearly nine o'clock before he called for me. He was in a very bad temper and gave me sharp cuts with the whip although I was going at full speed. The road was stony, and before we were out of the town my shoe came off. But Smith was too drunk to notice.

My shoeless foot suffered dreadfully. The hoof was broken and split, and the inside was cut by the sharp stones. I could not go on, because the pain was too great. I stumbled, and fell violently on both my knees. Smith was flung off and landed with great force.

I soon recovered my feet and limped to the side of the road. I could see Smith lying a few yards beyond me. He made one effort to get up but couldn't, then groaned and lay still.

It must have been nearly midnight when I heard a horse's feet, the wheels of the dog-cart, and men's voices. I neighed loudly and was overjoyed to hear an answering neigh from Ginger. They came slowly over the stones and stopped.

One of the men jumped down beside the dark figure on the ground. "It's Reuben!" he said. "He doesn't move!"

"He's dead," said the other man. "Feel how cold his hands are. And his head is covered with blood."

Then they saw my cut knees.

"Why, the horse fell and threw him!" one said. "Look, his hoof is cut to pieces. No wonder he went down, riding over these stones without a shoe! Reuben must have been drunk to ride a horse without a shoe."

He tied his handkerchief round my foot and they led me slowly home.

I was cleared of all blame for the accident. The ostler at the White Lion, and several other people, said that Reuben Smith was drunk when he left the inn.

But I had to leave Earlshall, and so did Ginger. She had been ruined by hard riding and was to be sold. And although my knees healed, they did not look nice enough for his lordship. So one day Robert came into the field where I was with Ginger and took me away. We were both very sad to say goodbye to each other, Ginger and I.

I was bought by the master of a livery stables where I was a 'job horse' and was hired out to all kinds of people. Then one man took a special liking to me and persuaded my master to sell me to a friend of his who wanted a safe, pleasant horse for riding.

And so that summer I was sold to Mr. Barry.

Mr. Barry knew very little about horses, but he hired a comfortable stable for me and a man called Filcher as a groom. He ordered the best hay, oats, crushed beans and bran, so there was plenty of good food and I thought I was well off.

For a few days all went well, but after a while it seemed to me that there were fewer oats in my meals. I had the beans, but bran was mixed in with them instead of oats. In two or three weeks this began to tell on my strength and spirits. However, I could not say anything and it went on for about two months.

One afternoon my master rode into the country to see a gentleman farmer who happened to know about horses. The farmer looked closely at me.

"It seems to me that your horse doesn't look as well as he did when you first had him, Barry," he said.

"My groom says that horses are always dull and weak in the autumn, and that I must expect it," said my master.

"Fiddlesticks!" said the farmer. "Why this is only August! And with your light work and the good food, he ought not to be like this." He put a hand over my neck and shoulder. "He's as warm and wet as a horse that's just come up from grass. I advise you to look into your stable a little more. There are scoundrels wicked enough to rob a horse of his food."

I could have told my master where his oats went to. My groom came every morning at six o'clock, with his little boy. The boy carried a basket and went into the room where the oats were kept. I would see them filling a bag with oats and putting it into the basket.

Five or six mornings after the visit to the farmer, the boy left the stable with his basket of oats, but came back soon after, looking frightened. Two policemen came with him.

"Show me where your father keeps the food for his chickens," one policeman said to the boy.

The boy began to cry but there was no escape. Moments later, the policemen found another empty bag like the one in the boy's basket, and they took Filcher away with them. I heard afterwards that the boy was not held to be guilty, but the man was sent to prison for two months.

A new groom was employed, but he didn't clean the stable properly and my feet became unhealthy from standing on wet straw. After treatment, I was soon well again, but Mr. Barry was so disgusted at being twice deceived by his grooms that he decided to give up keeping a horse. So I was sent to a horse fair where I was bought for twenty five pounds by a man called Jeremiah Barker.

CHAPTER 9

A London Cab Horse

Jerry Barker was a small man but well-built and quick in all his movements. I knew by the way he handled me that he was used to horses. He spoke gently and there was a clean, fresh smell about him that made me take to him.

Jerry lived in London and was a cab driver. His wife Polly was a plump, trim, tidy, little woman with smooth, dark hair, dark eyes and a merry little mouth. His son Harry was nearly twelve years old and was a tall, good-tempered boy. His daughter Dolly was eight, and she looked just like her mother. They were all wonderfully fond of each other.

Jerry had his own cab and two horses which he drove and groomed himself. His other horse was a tall, white, large-boned animal called Captain. The next morning after Jerry bought me, Polly and Dolly came to see me. Harry had helped his father since early that morning and had already decided that I would be a good horse. Polly brought me a slice of apple and Dolly brought me some bread.

"We'll call him Jack after the old one, shall we, Polly?" said Jerry.

"Do," she said. "I like to keep a good name going."

Captain went out in the cab all morning and I went in the afternoon. Jerry made sure that my collar and bridle were comfortable, and there was no bearing rein. What a blessing that was!

After driving through a side-street we came to the large cab-stand where the other cabs were drawn up. We took our place behind the last cab. Two or three men came to look at me and pass remarks.

"Very good for a funeral," said one.

"Too smart-looking," said another. "You'll find something wrong with him one of these fine mornings."

Then a broad-faced man came up. He was dressed in a great grey coat with capes and white buttons, a grey hat, and a scarf tied around his neck. His hair was grey, too, but he was a jolly-looking fellow, and the other men made way for him. This man's name was Grant, but he was called "Governor Grant". He had been on the stand the longest of all the men.

He looked me all over. "He's the right sort for you, Jerry," he said. "I don't care what you gave for him, he'll be worth it."

My first week as a cab horse was very trying. I was not used to London and its noise, hurry, and crowds of horses, carts and carriages. But I soon found that I could trust my driver, and Jerry discovered that I was willing to work and do my best. He never laid the whip on me, and in a short time we understood each other as well as a horse and man can.

Jerry kept his horses clean, gave us plenty of food and fresh water, and on Sundays we rested. He was kind and good-tempered, like John Manly. And he could not bear people who were always late and who wanted a cab horse to be driven hard to make up for their idleness.

One day, two wild-looking young men came out of a tavern and called to him, "Here, cabby! Look sharp, we're late! Put on the steam and get us

to Victoria in time for the one o'clock train. If you do, you shall have a shilling extra!"

"I will take you at the regular pace, gentlemen," said Jerry. "Shillings don't pay for putting on the steam like that."

Larry's cab was standing next to ours. He flung open the door and said, "I'm your man, gentlemen! My horse will get you there all right." And he shut them in with a wink at Jerry. "It's against his conscience to go faster than a jog-trot!" Then, whipping his horse hard, he set off as fast as he could.

Jerry patted me on the neck. "No, Jack, a shilling wouldn't pay for that sort of thing, would it, old boy?"

Although he was against hard driving to please careless people, he always went at a fair pace and was not against putting on the steam if there was a good reason.

I well remember one morning we were on the stand waiting for a fare. A young man carrying a large suitcase slipped on a piece of orange-peel and fell down heavily. Jerry was first to run and help him up, and then he took him into a shop to sit him down.

Ten minutes later, the young man came out again and called Jerry. We drew up by the pavement.

"Can you take me to the South-Eastern Railway?" he said. "My fall has made me late, and it's very important that I don't miss the twelve o'clock train. I'll gladly pay you an extra fare."

"I'll do my very best," said Jerry.

It is always difficult to drive fast in the city in the middle of the day when the streets are full of traffic. But no one could beat Jerry and I when it came to getting through the carriages and carts, vans and buses. In and out, in and out we went, as fast as a horse can do it. And we whirled into the station as the big clock pointed to eight minutes to twelve.

"We're in time!" said the young man. "Thank you, my friend, and your good horse, too. You've saved me more than money can ever pay. Take this extra half-crown."

"No, sir, thank you all the same," said Jerry. "I'm glad we were in time. Now hurry and catch your train."

When we got back to the cab-stand, there was a good deal of laughing because Jerry had driven hard to the train. The other drivers wanted to know how much extra fare he'd pocketed.

"The gentleman offered me an extra half-crown, but I didn't take it," said Jerry. "If Jack and I choose to have a quick run now and then, that's our business and not yours."

Poor Ginger

One day, while our cab and many others were waiting outside one of the London parks, a shabby, old cab drove up beside ours. The horse was an old, worn-out chestnut with an ill-kept coat and bones that showed plainly through it. I'd been eating some hay and the wind rolled a little of it her way. The poor creature put out her long, thin neck and picked it up, then turned and looked for more. There was a hopeless look in her dull eye, and I was wondering where I'd seen her before when she looked straight at me.

"Black Beauty, is that you?" she said.

It was Ginger! But how she had changed! The beautifully arched, glossy neck was now straight and lank and fallen in; the clean, straight legs were swollen, and the joints were grown out of shape with hard work; her face, which was once so full of life, was now full of suffering, and her breathing was very bad. I sidled up to her so that we could have a quiet talk, and it was a sad tale that she had to tell.

After twelve months rest at Earlshall she was considered to be fit for work again, and was sold to a gentleman. For a little while she got on well. But after a longer gallop than usual, the old strain returned and, after

being rested and doctored, she was sold again. In this way, she changed hands several times but always got lower down.

"I was bought by this man who keeps a number of cabs and horses, and hires them out," said Ginger. "You look well off, and I'm glad, but it's different for me. They whip me and work me seven days a week with not one thought about what I suffer. They say that I'm not worth what they paid for me, so they're working me until they get their money back."

"You used to stand up for yourself if you were ill-used," I said.

"Ah, I did once," said Ginger. "But it's no use. Men are strongest, and if they're cruel and have no feelings, then there's nothing we can do except bear it. I wish the end would come. I wish I was dead."

I was very much troubled, and I put my nose against hers. But I could find nothing to say to comfort her. I think she was pleased to see me because she said, "You're the only friend I ever had."

A short time after this, a cart with a dead horse in it passed our cab-stand. The head hung out of the cart-tail and it was a chestnut horse with a long, thin neck. I believe it was Ginger. I hoped it was, for then her troubles would be over.

On election day there was no lack of work for Jerry and me. First came a stout, puffy gentleman with a carpet bag; he wanted to go to Bishopsgate Station. Then we were called by a lady who wanted to be taken to Regent's Park; and later a man jumped into the cab and called out, "Bow Street Police Station, quick!"

After another journey or two, we came back to the cab-stand. Jerry put on my nose-bag and said, "We must eat when we can on days like this, Jack." And he took out one of Polly's meat pies and began to eat it.

But we hadn't eaten many mouthfuls before a poor, young woman carrying a heavy child, came along the street. She looked quite bewildered and came up to Jerry to ask him the way to St Thomas' hospital. She had to take her child there.

"He's suffering a great deal of pain," she said. "But the doctor says that if I can get him to the hospital then he could get well. Which way is it, sir?"

"You can't carry him through the crowds," said Jerry. "It's three miles away, and that child is too heavy. You could be knocked down. Just get into this cab and I'll drive you to the hospital. Don't you see the rain is coming on?"

"I can't do that, sir," she said. "I've only just enough money to get back with. Please tell me the way."

"Look here, missus," said Jerry. "I've got a wife and dear children at home, and I know a father's feelings. Now get in the cab and I'll take you for nothing."

"Heaven bless you!" said the woman, and she burst into tears.

As Jerry went to open the door, two men with colours in their hats and button-holes ran up calling, "Cab!"

"Engaged," cried Jerry. But one man pushed past the woman and jumped in, followed by the other. Jerry looked as stern as a policeman. "This cab is already engaged, gentlemen, by this lady."

"Lady!" said one of them. "Oh, she can wait. Our business is very important. Besides we were in first and we'll stay in."

A smile came over Jerry's face as he shut the cab door. "All right, gentlemen, stay as long as it suits you. I can wait while you rest yourselves." He turned his back on them and walked over to the young woman who was standing near me. "They'll soon be gone, don't worry," he said, laughing.

And they soon were gone; for when they understood Jerry's dodge, they got out, calling him all sorts of bad names. After this, we were soon on our way to the hospital.

"Thank you a thousand times," said the young woman as Jerry helped

her out of the cab.

"You're welcome, and I hope the dear child will soon be better," said Jerry. He watched her go in, then patted my neck, which was something he always did when anything pleased him.

The rain was coming down fast and, just as we were leaving the hospital, a lady came down the steps calling, "Cab!" and Jerry seemed to know her at once.

"Jerry Barker, is it you?" said the woman. "I'm very glad to find you here. You're just the friend I want. It's very difficult to get a cab in this part of London today."

"I shall be proud to serve you, ma'am," said Jerry. "Where may I take you?"

"To Paddington Station," said the woman.

We got to the station in good time and, being under shelter, the lady stood talking to Jerry. I found she had once been Polly's mistress.

"How do you find cab work suits you in the winter?" she asked Jerry. "I know Polly was anxious about your cough last year."

"She worries herself a good deal. You see, ma'am, I work all hours and in all kinds of weather. But I get on pretty well and I'd feel quite lost without horses to look after."

"It would be a pity to seriously risk your health in this work, not only for your own sake but for Polly and the children's as well," she said. "There are many places where good drivers or grooms are wanted. If you ever think of giving up cab work, let me know." She put something into his hand. "There's five shillings each for the children. Polly will know how to spend it."

Jerry thanked her and, after leaving the station, we went home.

Christmas and the New Year are very merry times for some people, but for the cabmen and their horses, it is no holiday. There are so many parties and places of amusement open that the work is often hard and late. Sometimes driver and horse have to wait for hours in the rain or frost, shivering with cold.

We had a great deal of late work Christmas week, and Jerry's cough was bad. But however late we were, Polly sat up waiting for him, looking anxious and troubled.

On New Year's Eve we had to take two gentlemen to a house in one of the West End Squares, and were told to come for them at eleven o'clock. "You may have to wait a few minutes, but don't be late," one of them said.

As the clock struck eleven we were at the door, for Jerry was always punctual. The clock chimed the quarter hours, then struck midnight, but the door did not open. The wind was sharp with driving sleet. Jerry pulled one of my cloths higher over my neck. He then walked up and down,

stamping his feet and beating his arms, but that set him off coughing.

At half-past twelve, Jerry rang the door-bell and asked the servant if he would be wanted that night.

"Oh, yes, you'll be wanted," said the man.

At a quarter-past one the door opened and the two men came out. They got in the cab without a word and told Jerry where to drive. It was nearly two miles away, and when the men got out they didn't say they were sorry to have kept us waiting so long. Instead they were angry when Jerry charged them for the extra time. But it was hard-earned money to Jerry.

At last we got home. Jerry could hardly speak, and his cough was dreadful. But he gave me a rub down as usual and even put down an extra bundle of straw for my bed. Polly brought me a warm mash that made me comfortable, and then they locked the door.

It was late the next morning before anyone came, and then it was only Harry. He cleaned us, fed us, swept out the stalls, then put the straw back again, as if it was Sunday. At noon he came again and gave us our food and water, and this time Dolly came with him. She was crying, and I gathered from what they said that Jerry was dangerously ill.

Two days passed, and we only saw Harry and Dolly. On the third day, Governor Grant arrived when Harry was in the stable.

"I wouldn't go to the house, my boy," he said, "but I want to know how your father is."

"He's very bad," said Harry. "They call it bronchitis. The doctor thinks it will turn one way or the other tonight."

"That's very bad," said Mr. Grant. "But while there's life there's hope, so keep your spirits up."

Early next morning, he came again.

"Well?" he said.

"Father is better," said Harry. "Mother hopes he will get over it soon."

"Thank God!" said Governor Grant.

Jerry grew better steadily, but the doctor said he must never go back to the cab work again if he wished to be an old man. The children talked a lot about what their mother and father would do, but a few days later Dolly ran into the stable to find Harry.

"Mother's got a letter from Mrs. Fowler, her old mistress!" said Dolly. "She says we're all to go and live near her in the country. There's an empty cottage that will just suit us. Her coachman is going away in the spring and then she'll want father in his place!"

And so it was quickly settled that as soon as Jerry was well enough, they would move to the country. The cab and the horses would be sold.

This was heavy news for me, for I was not young and could not hope for a better place, although Governor Grant promised to do his best for me.

The day came for going away. Jerry had not been allowed to go out yet, and I never saw him after that New Year's Eve. Polly and the children came to say goodbye.

"Dear Jack," said Polly. "I wish we could take you with us." And so I was led away to my new place.

CHAPTER 11

Hard Times

I was sold to a corn dealer and baker whom Jerry knew and then to another cab owner whose name was Nicholas Skinner. He had black eyes and a hook nose and he was hard on his drivers. In this place we had no Sunday rest, and it was the heat of the summer. Sometimes on a Sunday morning, a party of men would hire the cab for the day. Four of them sat inside and another sat with the driver. I had to take them ten or fifteen miles out into the country and back again. Never would any of them walk up a hill, even on the hottest day, and sometimes I was so fevered and worn that I could hardly touch my food.

My driver had a cruel whip with something so sharp at the end that it sometimes drew blood. But I still did my best and never hung back. As Ginger had said, it was no use – men are the strongest.

My life was now so wretched that I wished I was dead like poor Ginger. And one day I nearly got my wish.

We were waiting outside the railway station when a party of four people called for us – a noisy, blustering man with a lady, a little boy, a young girl, and a great deal of luggage. The lady and the boy got into the cab, and while the man gave orders about the luggage, the girl came and looked at me.

"Papa," she said, "I'm sure this poor horse cannot take us and our luggage so far. He's very weak and tired."

"Oh, he's all right, miss!" said my driver. "He's strong enough." And he put up a box so heavy that I could feel the springs go down.

"Papa, Papa, do take a second cab," pleaded the young girl. "I'm sure this is very cruel."

"Nonsense, Grace. Get in at once, and don't make all this fuss," said her father. "The driver knows his own business."

My gentle friend had to obey, and box after box was dragged up and lodged on the top of the cab, or settled by the side of the driver. At last all was ready, and with his usual jerk at the rein and slash of the whip, the driver drove me off.

The load was very heavy, and I'd had neither food nor rest since the morning. But I did my best and got along fairly well until we came to Ludgate Hill. But there the heavy load and my own exhaustion were too much for me. My feet slipped from under me and I fell heavily to the ground, knocking all the breath out of my body. I lay perfectly still – indeed I could not move, and thought I was going to die.

I heard loud, angry voices around me, and luggage was taken off the cab. But it was all like a dream. I thought I heard the girl's voice saying, "Oh, that poor horse! It's all our fault!"

Someone loosened my bridle and collar. Another said, "He's dead, he'll never get up again." Then I heard a policeman giving orders, but I did not open my eyes. Some cold water was thrown over my head, and some cordial was poured into my mouth. Something was put over me. I cannot tell how long I lay there, but I found life coming back to me, and a kind-voiced man was patting me and encouraging me to rise. After one or two attempts, I staggered to my feet. Then I was gently led to some stables close by.

That evening I was taken back to Skinner's stables, and the next

morning the farrier came to examine me.

"This is a case of overwork more than disease," he said. "There's not an ounce of strength left in him."

"Then he must just go to the dogs," said Skinner. "I've no meadows to nurse sick horses. That sort of thing doesn't suit my business. My plan is to work 'em as long as they'll go, then sell them for what they'll fetch at the knacker's or elsewhere."

"There's a sale of horses in ten days," said the farrier. "If you rest him and feed him up, he may improve, and you may get more than his skin's worth at any rate."

Reluctantly, Skinner took this advice and gave orders that I should be well-fed and cared for. This did more to improve my condition than anything else could have done. I was taken to the sale a few miles out of London. I felt that any change must be an improvement, and I held up my head and hoped for the best.

CHAPTER 12

My Last Home

At this sale I found myself in company with the old, broken-down horses, some of which it would have been merciful to shoot. The buyers and sellers did not look much better off than the poor beasts they were bargaining for.

Then I noticed a man who looked like a gentleman farmer, with a young boy at his side. They came over to me.

"There's a horse that's known better days, Willie," said the man.

"Poor old fellow," said the boy. "Grandpa, do you think he was ever a carriage horse?"

"Oh, yes, my boy!" said the man. "There's a good deal of breeding about that horse." He put out a hand and gave me a kind pat on the neck. I put out my nose in answer to his kindness, and the boy stroked my neck.

"See, Grandpa, how he understands kindness! Won't you buy him?"

The man who was selling me said, "The young gentleman knows a good horse when he sees one, sir. This one 'ere is just pulled down with overwork. He's not an old one. It would be worth a gentleman's while to give a five pound note for him and let him have a chance. Why, he'll be worth twenty next spring!"

The old gentleman laughed and the boy looked up eagerly. Five pounds in sovereigns changed hands, and soon after I was gently ridden home by a servant of my new master's and put into a large meadow with a shed in one corner of it.

Mr. Thoroughgood, for that was the name of the farmer, gave orders that I should have hay and oats every night and morning, and a run of the meadow every day.

"And you, Willie, can be in charge of him," he said.

The boy was proud of his charge and there was not a day when he did not pay me a visit. He always came with a kind word and I grew very fond of him.

During the winter, my legs improved so much that I began to feel quite young again. Then the spring came round and Mr. Thoroughgood decided to try me in the phaeton. I was well-pleased and did the work with perfect ease.

"He's growing young, Willie," he said. "We must give him a little gentle work now and look for a quiet home for him where he will be valued."

One day during this summer, the groom cleaned and dressed me with great care. Willie seemed half-anxious and half-merry as he got into the chaise with his grandfather.

"I hope the ladies like him," said the old gentleman.

A mile or two from the village, we came to a pretty house with a lawn and shrubbery at the front and a drive up to the door. Willie rang the bell and asked if Miss Blomefield or Miss Ellen were at home. As they were, Willie stayed with me while Mr. Thoroughgood went into the house.

In about ten minutes he returned, followed by three ladies. One tall, pale lady, wrapped in a white shawl was leaning on a younger woman, with dark eyes and a merry face. The other, a very stately-looking person, was Miss Blomefield.

"If you like," said Mr Thoroughgood, "you can have him on trial, and then your coachman will see what he thinks of him."

"Your recommendation will go a long way with me," said the stately lady. "We will accept your offer of a trial."

It was then arranged that I should be sent for the next day, and in the morning a smart-looking young man came for me. At first he looked pleased, but when he saw my knees he said, "I didn't think you would recommend a blemished horse like that."

"You are only taking him on trial," said my master. "If he's not as safe as any horse you ever drove, send him back."

I was led home, placed in a comfortable stable, fed, and left to myself. The next day, the groom was cleaning my face when he said, "That's just like the star Black Beauty had on his forehead. He's much the same height, too. I wonder where Black Beauty is now." He began to look me over carefully, talking to himself. "White star on the forehead, one white foot on the off side – and that little patch of white hair on his back! It must be Black Beauty! Why, Beauty! Do you know me? I'm little Joe Green, who almost killed you!" And he began patting and patting me as if he was overjoyed.

I could not say I remembered him, for he was now a fine-grown young fellow with black whiskers and a man's voice. But I was sure he knew me and that he was Joe Green, and I was very glad. I put my nose up to him and tried to say that we were friends. I never saw a man so pleased!

"Give you a fair trial!" he said. "I should think so indeed! I wish John Manly was here to see you."

In the afternoon I was put into a low Park chair and brought to the door. Miss Ellen was going to try me, and Joe went with her. I heard him telling her about me and that he was sure I was Squire Gordon's old Black Beauty.

"I shall certainly write to Mrs. Gordon and tell her that her favourite horse has come to us," she said. "How pleased she will be!"

I have now lived in this happy place for a whole year. Joe is the best and kindest of grooms. My work is easy and pleasant, and I feel my strength and spirits all coming back again.

My ladies have promised that they will never sell me, and so I have nothing to fear. And here my story ends. My troubles are all over, and I am at home. And often, before I am quite awake, I fancy I am still in the orchard at Birtwick, standing with my old friends under the apple trees.